LILY AND THE BEARS

BY CHRISTINE ROSS

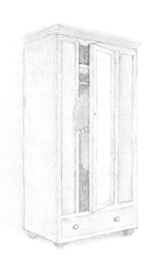

Houghton Mifflin Company
Boston 1991

LILY didn't like being a child. "I want to be something big and brave," she said to herself. "I want to be a big tough wild bear." So every morning instead of putting on her clothes she put on her wild bear suit.

L ILY's father didn't like living with a wild bear. It always gave him a bit of a shock to see a bear in the bathroom.

LILY's mother didn't like having a bear for a child because it always growled at the visitors, and they never came back.

LILY's grandmother didn't like having a bear about the house either. "In the good old days when I was a girl," she would say, "children were children and bears were bears."

ONE day Lily's class went to the zoo. Lily couldn't wait to see the other wild bears.

They saw the giraffe and the rhinoceros, the monkeys and the hippopotamus, the panther, the python and the platypus.

AND they all went for a ride on the elephant. The elephant was very suspicious of Lily.

WHEN it was time to go, Lily was so busy admiring the bears that she got left behind. This was a disaster because a near-sighted keeper mistook her for a real bear.

POOR Lily was caught and locked in with the real wild bears.

"Hello, what's this?" said a very large bear, sharpening his claws. "It must be lunchtime."

"I'm a wild bear too," said Lily.

"Don't be ridiculous," said the bear. "I know a bear when I see one. Real bears don't have zippers down their fronts."

"THIS cage is only for real bears," growled the bears. "No fakes allowed. Get out." They all began to roar and gnash their big white teeth.

"Help help," yelled Lily.

"CAN'T you bears be quiet?" said the keeper.

"I'm not a bear. Let me out!" shouted Lily. "I'm a child. See . . ." and she pulled off her bear suit.

"Who'd want to be a bear? Bears are mean and nasty. I want to go home."

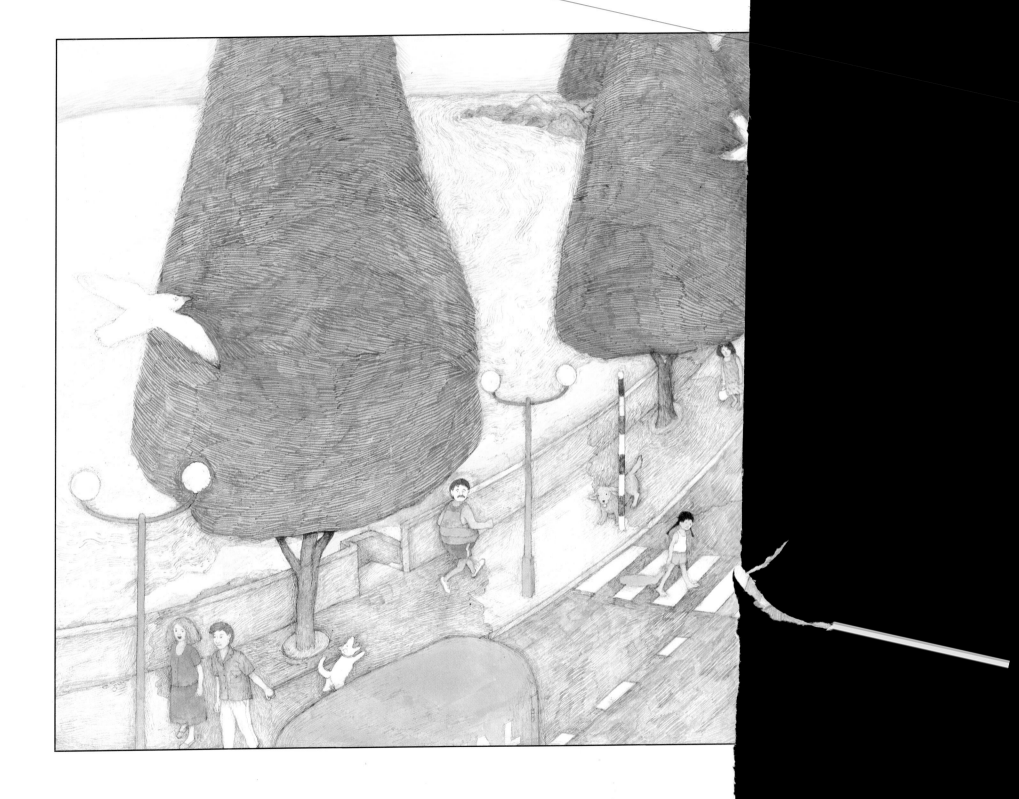

L ILY'S mother and father heaved great sighs of relief when Lily came home dragging her bear suit behind her. "We're so glad to have an ordinary child again," they said.

But . . .

THE next morning when Lily got up she didn't put on her ordinary child clothes.

"Deep sea divers are big and brave," she said as she put on her flippers and snorkel. "That's what I'll be."